Short SF Stories

Dimensions

of

Dread and Delight

by

Jane Palmer

Dodo Books
www.booksfromdodo.uk

The Stories

The Buddha of Rebirth

There were faint strains of music in the distance and shadowy forms flitted past the frosted panels of the observation booth.

Nothing out of the ordinary so far.

Unit One beeped the all clear to Unit Two and they unfolded their multi-jointed limbs.

After a quick air pressure check the androids strode out into the chaotic world they were charged with monitoring.

Life forms here had long since ceased to pay attention to the mechanical spies amongst them; they would have probably been missed if not seen on their regular rounds.

A beefy semi-clad primate grunted as they passed. It might have been a greeting or abuse. Units One and

1

Two had never been able to calculate the difference. Even the distant music baffled their limited audio circuits, but they headed towards it all the same, through the chaos of the crowded valley and towards the temple at its far end.

The huge effigy of the smiling deity at the entrance raised the palm of a hand in greeting.

They stepped inside.

'What will it be today, friends?' asked the wizened devotee sitting cross-legged before the altar alight with joss sticks.

Unit One raised seven digits of a hand.

'Well... If you can handle it...' The old man in the faded saffron robe filled a small pressurised canister and handed it to Unit One who swished the dial on its palm over the screen he offered.

'And for you?' Unit Two was asked, but responded with a closed fist. 'I see. One of you has to keep its circuits clear to go on monitoring us I suppose.'

The huge, smiling deity waved as they left and the music descended from the clouds, enveloping their sensors with comforting chaotic melodies which had such a soporific effect on the inhabitants of this weird world.

Completing their regular inspections, the units headed to the safety of their observation booth pressurised against the catastrophe that happened every evening when the bustling surroundings began to disintegrate. They sealed themselves in as the inhabitants, houses and temples of the world outside were reduced to the germ of what they had been during that day.

Unit One injected the canister of narcotic into its cerebral processor, and then drifted into a circuit deadening torpor.

Unit Two stayed alert until the morning explosion of sunlight struck the frosted windows of their quantum secure sanctuary.

Still numb from the after effects of the drug, Unit One watched its companion monitor the disconcerting rebirth of a city that had no scientific explanation.

Every morning, the floating detritus that had the day before been living creatures and the constructions they lived in were restored. Seeing everything refleshed and brought back to life was the part even a machine had trouble dealing with. Not because of the implausibly unpleasant process, but because there was no logical explanation for it.

Somehow, somewhere back in the mists of time when the rest of the planet had been devastated by a cosmic cataclysm, this small community remained suspended in perpetual rebirth. Beyond the valley lay the blasted, world-wide wasteland Units One and Two had been dispatched to monitor from the signals of satellites orbiting above, as well as observing the surviving city and its inhabitants.

But this time, when the restoration was almost complete, the planet trembled.

Units One and Two left their secure booth to find out what was happening.

As seismometers registered shock waves emanating from its unstable core the planet shuddered like some huge, hairy beast shaking an ocean from its fur.

All communications severed, Units One and Two could only stand and wonder at the worldwide catastrophe about to put an end to the perpetual metamorphoses of the city and its inhabitants.

Was this a rerun of the disaster which the repeatedly reborn population had been saved from? Or a cosmic step back to its original state?

Then, with one final shudder, the planet ponderously disintegrated.

Still unable to compute what was happening, Units One and Two found themselves floating in space with its debris.

Not programmed to deal with this eventuality, they started to drift away from each other. All their computing power and sophisticated components could do nothing about it. At least Unit One still had enough narcotics swilling about in its system to avoid being unduly bothered, while Unit Two frantically sent out distress signals on all wavelengths in the hope someone or something might intercept them. It was probably futile, yet filled time before all its circuits ran down.

But Unit Two's call for help was received.

Like a large luminous cloud, the amiable deity that had guarded the temple loomed into view. A friendly, beaming moon that raised its palm with the promise of rebirth.

Maisie May

Maisie May was a happy soul, always out and about
with her small yapping terrier, chatting to magpies
and anyone would stop and listen. She lived in a large
house on the hill. Some said it looked like Bates Motel,
others that it was the sort of residence with a view
they had always aspired to.

But, for all her sociability, no one had ever seen
inside it: even the window cleaner couldn't peer
through the heavy net and half drawn curtains.

Maisie May was probably no more than a solitary
eccentric of course, too fit and independent to allow
anyone over her threshold. She was spic and span, not

always making sense, and sometimes looked as though she was about to topple over, yet had not been known to. Despite pushing a four-wheeled shopping trolley, she had never been seen in a shop or hauling it on and off buses, though she must have been eligible for a bus pass. Her usual route was down to the park where she would talk to the ducks, though never feed them because her terrier became uncharacteristically subdued if one approached it. This, from a breed prepared to take on dogs ten times its size was strange as well. But then, people were so used to the odd couple they seldom stopped to wonder, just passed by with a brief, polite 'Hello'.

So Maisie May would sit on the seat by the lake and gaze into the distance when not chatting to pigeons or smiling at small children who smiled back warily as though able to see something about the old lady adults couldn't.

Her neighbours were aware that she had a carer or companion, though they were seldom seen together. Evidently Maisie was trusted out by herself when reasonably coherent and safely balanced by her shopping trolley.

Given that she was never seen buying anything, some wondered what weighty object was being trundled about with her everywhere. One old man reckoned he heard it make an odd clicking sound, but had put it down to tinnitus. Perhaps, if people had dared to get closer to Maisie, they might have heard a faint whirring as well.

It was one of those muggy days when the humidity was intense enough to warp doors and the lake lay still, not betraying its treacherous depth. Mothers brought their infants to look at the ducks and let them skip across a narrow bridge with a railing too low to prevent a small pixie toppling into the water.

Maisie May sat gazing, intent on some point in the distance, while the ducks huddled together on the damp grass.

There was a splash, and then silence.

That was no duck taking to the water. It was a child, noiselessly splashing about, choking and unable to call out to his mother deep in gossip with two others.

There was a "click".

Maisie's head turned as though detecting an incoming missile.

Only then did the mother notice her drowning child and begin wailing in futility. She couldn't swim, neither could her companions.

But Maisie May could.

She suddenly stood bolt upright and dived into the lake like a spear.

The young women screamed even louder, barely making sense to the emergency services they were phoning.

Maisie, after disappearing for a while, suddenly surfaced supporting the panicking child so he could breathe. For a moment it looked as though she was unable to take her bearings.

Then her seldom seen carer dashed down the hill to the lake. In her hand was a control unit. As she deftly operated its lever, Maisie turned, keeping the child above the water, and brought him to the bank. His mother snatched him to safety, hardly glancing at the elderly woman who had saved her son's life.

Maisie hadn't fared so well.

Her electronics were waterlogged, and even trying to use the battery in the shopping trolley to reboot her was of no avail. The paramedics who had rushed to the scene could only stand and stare as the elderly patient was quickly disassembled and packed away, component by component into her shopping trolley.

Maisie's carer smiled at their astonishment. 'Still a problem with damp. We will have to encase the processors in something more waterproof.' Then she wheeled her creation back up to the house on the hill.

The small terrier tagged along robotically at her heels.

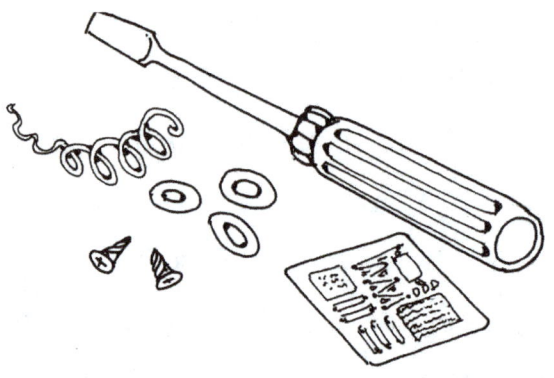

Mepple

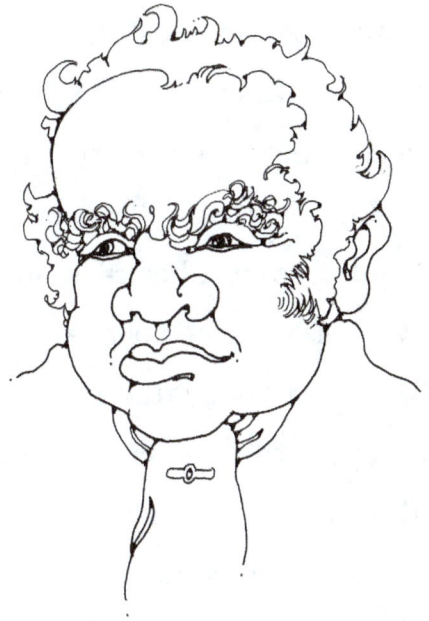

He was once large, repellent, and believed in his own superiority.

On first meeting him anyone would have been impressed by this loquacious, evidently companionable, bladder full of words and points of view that made the more open-minded cringe.

There he used to go, admiring his reflection in shop windows as though he had shares in every other one. That might have been true a decade ago, but any charisma associated with power had dwindled away with the influence the privileged felt that they had a right to. The pompous man had never come to terms with being a nonentity, possibly because no one wanted to hear how it had happened. Oddly enough, they might have been interested, if only for the wrong reason. Now there was a vacuous look in those rheumy eyes, as though some other entity was sharing the same space.

Mepple had produced books on ancient history, edited and written articles for prestigious publications, and mixed with Eton-educated intelligentsia like him. This and dealing with less privileged mortals who were obliged to work for a living had been so condescending it was a wonder someone hadn't hit him, but he had always somehow managed to get away with it.

So what did happen to drop this important man into genteel penury and account for that distant look in his eyes? Bad investment? Family death duties? Run-in with the law?

Nothing so pedestrian.

He had made the mistake of trying to impress the wrong person.

Unaware of how repellent he was so many years ago, and when he looked more affluent, he had made an attempt to engage an attractive young woman in conversation.

That same self-regard also resulted in him failing to notice that much younger and more suitable men were deliberately avoiding her as she navigated the hotel lounge. They probably weren't sure why, but those huge, dark eyes that would have been appealing on an antelope were too large, the ivory skin was too taut, and the voluptuous smile bordered on the glassy.

Pumped up by his own ego, how could this amazing creature resist Mepple?

His first approach went well enough: drinks on the hotel patio as the sun went down, and then an evening meal. After that, before he could make the inevitable proposition, she invited him for a stroll under the brightly shining moon. Had he been aware of why most women avoided him, alarm bells might have rung then, but full moons held no terror for him, nor did he believe in vampires or zombies. They were the domain of his intellectual colleagues who eulogised Tolkien and conversed in Elfish. Mepple's was a self-assured world where the fantasist and gullible had no place... unfortunately for him.

As they strolled, there was a rainbow halo around the moon as a veil of mist passed over it.

Then it started to turn red.

Had Mepple been interested in astronomy he would have realised that this was no eclipse where the Earth's shadow turned it into a blood moon. He paid it no attention, more focused on the tall, gorgeous woman loping beside him.

Loping?

Yes, her stride was becoming more animal by the moment, though what sort of animal he was unable to fathom. Having an exotic creature grace him with its company further excited Mepple's libido.

Were those finely formed features becoming just a little cat like? Or perhaps his imagination was running away with what strange delights the night had to offer.

She turned her huge, animal eyes to gaze into his expectant ones, which had obviously not been anticipating the object of his desire to turn into a dark, sinister cloud which enveloped him.

The transformation was too sudden for Mepple's alcohol dulled reflexes to take in. Even someone with an imagination could not have anticipated any shape-shifter having designs on their body, especially one like his.

But there was a reason for taking over this bladder of self regard. The creature needed to shed the voluptuous woman's body which was beginning to reveal signs of the entity inhabiting it, and move in different circles where its host would be kept at a safe distance and dismissed as unwanted company.

That would give it time to seek a more suitable host.

The husk of the beautiful woman was sloughed off as Mepple became its, strangely, unresisting host.

Perhaps it was an improvement.

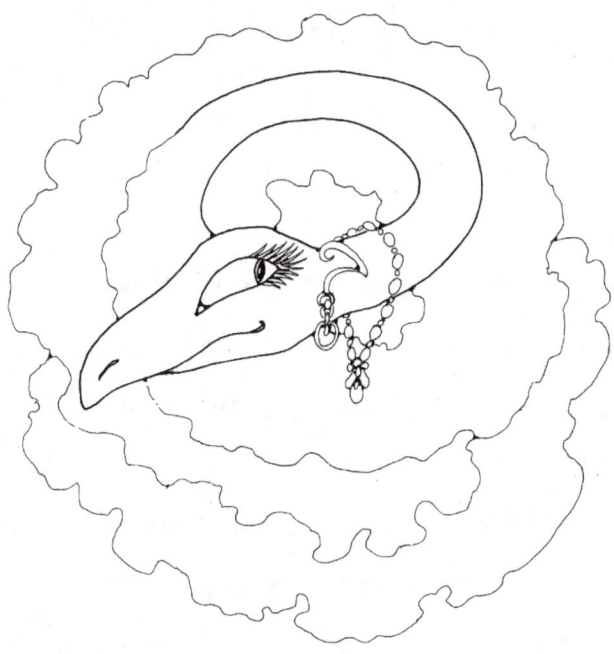

Wishful Dreams

It was a never-ending view so inviting any onlooker would have been persuaded that it was an optical illusion allowing them to see the mysterious lands beyond the horizon.

If it wasn't for that glorious anomaly, this world could have easily been a pristine Earth.

Gemma adjusted the power in her gravity boots so she could rise and see even further.

Then Graham started snoring.

A quick poke in the ribs and he stopped.

But it was too late. The beautiful dream would not let her back in. Once again the kitchen full of last night's washing-up lurched into her thoughts. The gravy in the plates wore mocking smiles and mugs clinked amongst themselves at a stupid joke they had no intention of letting her share.

So Gemma snatched up the nearest and hurled it at the window, which obligingly opened just in time. The crash of crockery on the patio woke her up... No, it was Graham snoring again. She should have been used to it by now.

There was nothing else for it, she would have to get up, make a cup of tea and take it out onto the patio to watch the sun rise.

This morning it seemed to be struggling as she sat back in the lounger and sipped from the mug that had been smashed to pieces in her kitchen dream.

Gemma pulled the smartphone from her dressing gown pocket to search "sunrise", only to discover that it was still two in the morning. So she switched it off and leaned back to doze.

Through the window of her catnap glowing shapes began to appear over the horizon.

'Oh good, they're back', Gemma heard herself murmur, though wasn't quite sure why.

The movement of the alien vehicles against the dark horizon was like a ballet. At least Graham's snoring wouldn't wake her up from this one.

A small craft, pulsating pink and yellow in turn landed daintily on the lawn. A spindly figure emerged and held up the palm of a three fingered hand in greeting.

Gemma reciprocated, 'Hi. Looking for some human specimens?'

Without speaking, the visitor might have been confirming her assumption.

'There is one snoring his head off upstairs,' she told the visitor. 'Won't be much use to you though. He's a useless so-and-so. Would never have married him, but back in those days there wasn't the choice.' As she heard herself speak, the craving to have at least a few years to herself grew more powerful. Oh that it could happen. After being married to a Jack the Lad who rapidly dwindled into a large lump of lard, the thought was too appealing for her to feel guilty about it.

The alien was gazing at her with diamond eyes, head tilted to one side as though interested.

'Oh, what's the point,' sighed Gemma, 'you're only a wishful dream.'

When Graham woke his first thought was to nudge his wife to get up and make some tea.

But Gemma wasn't there. The woman he believed to be part soul mate and part possession was nowhere in the house or garden. It was too early to go shopping, and bus passes weren't valid until after 9:30 anyway. She was 79 after all, so couldn't have gone far despite her many promises to leave him. She would have at least packed a change of clothes if she had, and their son was living in Canada, so she wouldn't be visiting him.

There was an empty mug on the patio. Gemma's smartphone lay beside it.

Then he noticed the circle of scorched grass in the lawn.

The horizon of the planet curved upwards, distorted by the dense atmosphere.

Gemma's pressurised suit allowed her to hang suspended above the jewel encrusted ground and be immersed in the glorious view.

Her new friends had promised her enough years to enjoy many more.

Until then, Gemma would not have believed that dreams came true. But then, she had spent most of her life living with Graham.

Patterns

Bands of colour crisscrossed the sky like a loosely woven cosmic basket.

This was not natural, any more than the text just received from a long dead friend.

Reality was changing - at least Christy Chan's was if no one else's. He was at that age when the thought of dementia looms large but, as this long dead friend had once assured him, when you've got the wits to assess the symptoms, you probably don't have it. Old age is compulsory and with luck you'll be gone before it turns to senility.

So why was Christy seeing intertwining streamers of colour pattern the sky?

When he looked again they were gone, so perhaps the hallucination was down to nothing more exotic than lack of sleep and gnawing feeling that he shouldn't really be there. He hadn't dared read that text: perhaps the long dead Jason was trying to explain something from the grave... or wherever he was now.

They never did find his body.

Perhaps Christy's changing perception of reality was the penalty for being so tough for so long. For all the battlefield scars and lost comrades, he'd never experienced the symptoms of post-traumatic stress. But then, he had never killed a civilian and had rescued too many to count, though that probably wasn't the point.

He did miss Jason, however; more than the two wives who had tried to domesticate him, which was probably another thing he should have thought more seriously about. There had never been time to bother with it before... heat of battle and all that.

So what now? Back to afternoon tea with the languorous Laura, or stroll round the park with her overweight poodle? The big decisions he used to make in an instant. Now, with all the time in the world, the small ones could take forever. Was it his turn to wash the dishes..?

There was a voice whispering at the back of his mind, 'Stop being such a twerp, Christy. There's no need for this.'

It was Jason's voice.

He tried not to listen, but it went on, 'They're all safe, man. You can come back now.'

Christy suddenly caught his breath and nearly toppled over. The brightly patterned sky was back. Now it was studded with flashes of light and the drone of huge wasps weaving in and out of the unravelling streamers of light.

Christy's knees gave way and refused to let him get up. It looked as though Petra the poodle would have to find her own way round the park that afternoon

The Jason he had heard was from decades ago, long before enforced retirement after one skirmish too many. Christy may have remained in uniform if he had chosen catering. But he needed to change the world for good, go out and protect people in war zones, see they reached somewhere, relatively, safe.

The next voice had an American accent. 'This was a mistake pal!'

'Too bloody true!' came back an angry Jason. 'Just help get those civilians out of here!'

The sky began to clear again. No more ribbons of light or low drone of monstrous insects.

The next voice was much quieter and female. 'Sorry Sir, nothing more we can do...'

Christy pulled himself up and at last opened the text from Jason. 'We will meet again old friend; not here, but some place yet to be discovered.'

And as he read, the words dissolved. The mobile faded from his hand and the brilliant sky descended to engulf him.

Christy Chan was posthumously awarded the Victoria Cross for putting himself between civilians and friendly fire.

Evolution

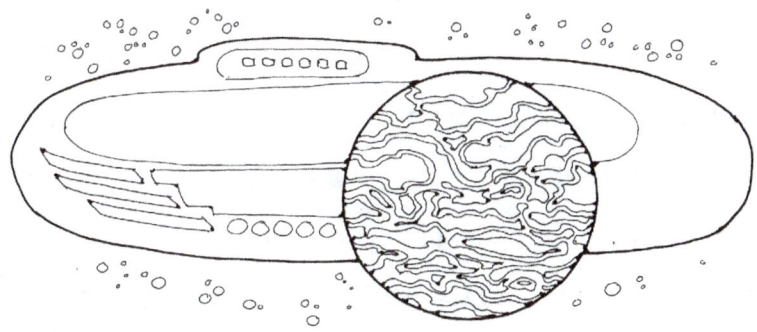

The sky hadn't always been blue: it used to be all the colours in a supernova, saturating everything in rainbow radiance as far as you could see.

Then came that strange entity, an oblong proto-moon moving purposefully towards the peaceful planet. Comets came and went in their huge elliptical orbits, describing slow moving trails across the dark sky on the rare occasions the triple suns were setting and sunsets of every hue illuminated the horizon. But this visitor was leaden, metallic and threatening.

There was the belief that matter changed and entropy would eventually render all things to the same boring level, and this monstrous interloper might have been its agent.

But this was not boring. It was dreadful... and blue. Not the blue of many skies lit by yellow suns, nor the chill hue of ice.

Long before its oppressive shadow fell over the planet, it was obvious that the threatening entity was no regular space debris. It was the size of several moons and held a precise position as it blocked the yellow sun's rays so its malign presence merged with the small blue star's. Despite being a red giant, the largest sun's corona was not strong enough to counteract it.

Signs of life were detected in the sinister visitor. Odd signals, incoherent and random, merged with the background transmissions of its smaller target world.

Long ago, the ancestors of the planet's inhabitants had discovered this lush, illuminated world and made it their own. The fact that an intelligent species already prospered on it did not trouble them. Technologically advanced and unable to comprehend the lives of more lowly (i.e. less technological) beings they exterminated the original population.

Under its new regime the planet blossomed into a flourishing, peace loving paradise. There was no need for envy here.

It was inevitable that this cosmic gem would attract the jealous attention of a species more technologically advanced and unable to understand the lives of its more lowly (less technological) population.

Train in the Trees to Insomniac Central

The train passed high above in the sky with no visible sign of support and plunged through a stand of trees before disappearing into the murky distance.

People should have been used to the sight by now, but still marvelled at the optical illusion created on those leaden, misty days that concealed the viaduct and everything bar movement. Some would sit at their front bedroom windows, fascinated by the sight. Others with jobs to go to just cursed the visibility and, instead of taking the car, got on the very trains causing such fascination. They always seemed to arrive more or less on time.

Ever since Bob had been an infant, they had been known as the ghost trains. Now he was much older, working long hours to pay the rent and suffering from insomnia. At least these trains were reliable, running their all stops service through the night, silently gliding high above on the viaduct in the early hours to pick up and drop late stragglers at each small station along the line. It was one of the few Beeching had dared not cut. Many thought it was because of the rumours that it was haunted, though more than likely because the trains served constituencies that the government risked losing had they tried to.

There was an old church next to one of the more isolated stations. It was rumoured that it had been taken over by a cult whose members depended on the late trains to attend the services, rituals, or whatever they got up to in the dead of night. The only ones in the vicinity who might have seen them come and go were badgers, but they were too busy fossicking to notice.

The church would have become derelict if that mysterious buyer had not bought it before the roof collapsed. Once deconsecrated, it could have been turned into a nightclub or wrestling venue for all the locals cared. There were no access roads and its old congregation had long since surrendered the nearest villages to second home buyers who had little interest in walking two miles to pray in its crumbling, damp interior.

Some insomniacs claimed that a phantom steam locomotive came and went in the early hours. It seemed to materialise from the shadow of the trees as though it had alighted on the viaduct from another dimension. This was probably a ghost train children believed in, while adults were disciplined enough to ignore the apparent evidence of their own eyes.

Then one night, as he lay wide awake gazing at the stars through half drawn curtains, Bob sat bolt upright, suddenly seized with the urge to follow the ghost train to the church. Despite being a ridiculous idea, he was unable to resist the impulse. He pulled on jeans over his pyjamas, threw on his padded jacket and went out to unlock his bicycle.

Unbeknown to Bob, other insomniacs across the region also inexplicably felt the urge to follow the steam billowing from the ghost train.

From the surrounding area more cyclists, also with overcoats over pyjamas, and one or two cars, found themselves converging on the remote church in the early hours. No one knew what had summoned them on that particular night. It might have been the luminous full moon or incongruous chuff chuff of a steam engine travelling on electrified rails that insisted that they leave the sweltering discomfort of their beds.

The interior of the church was well lit so, after some hesitation, Bob and the other visitors approached its open doors.

The phantom train was waiting at the nearby platform of the derelict branch station. Ghostly visitors disembarked from it and chatted to the mortal arrivals as though it was the most natural thing to do before entering the, almost, hallowed church.

The original pews had not been removed, so the congregation, mortal and ghostly, took their seats to listen to the imposing woman leaning over the pulpit above them.

She raised her hands in greeting. 'Welcome to Insomniac Central. All problems, pains and pettiness will not bother you in this place. Here the turbulent thoughts that keep you awake will dissolve away and filter back into the dimension they emanated from. Just take a pledge in these sanctified walls to be rid of them for good.'

Without hesitation the congregation, real and nebulous, raised their palms and fervently willed the ills that kept them awake not to return.

No local recalled peddling or driving back home, nor dreamer catching the ghost train. They just woke the next morning, refreshed for the first time they could remember as the stresses that had bedevilled their lives began to disappear.

The pay rise Bob thought he would never see, and desperately needed to pay his rising rent, was confirmed the next morning.

The troublesome teenagers that parents were unable to deal with unaccountably decided to move out or stop demanding money. The online trolls, vindictive business reviews by competitors and nuisance calls filtered away. More than one abusive boss had a stroke or heart attack, and the penalties on bank overdrafts were suddenly reduced.

Bob and a few others gratefully returned to the mysterious church.

It was dark and the doors bolted.

During that memorable night no one had noticed the effigy over the porch, a tall, imposing woman holding a full moon.

She had no name, just a title, "The Patron Saint of Insomniacs".

The Lychgate

There was a legend that the lychgate of the old church was the portal to the dimension of the undead. Given it was where bodies rested before being carried to their funeral, that seemed understandable enough. It could have been an ancient fable, though it was more likely invented by a customer hallucinating after tumbling out of the Red Lion opposite.

No one really believed that the dead left their purgatory to visit relatives or descendants, so the legend was safely relegated to horror stories in the playground and pamphlets on local hauntings.

Apart from briefly investigating how plausible the

legend might have been when trying to track down people who had gone missing over the years, the police also surreptitiously filed the stories under "fairytales".

But there was one detective who was determined to find a logical explanation for so many disappearances in that location.

Others lived for conspiracy theories. To them the lychgate held the only explanation for all those missing people last seen near it. After all, the church's crypt was reputedly linked to a maze of tunnels which could have led to a mini Minotaur, though were more likely ancient boltholes for persecuted clergy.

Like D I O'Connor, Dom was on the side of rational explanation and had the technology to disprove enough irrational theories to brand him as a killjoy nerd on several social media platforms. The one case that really gave him pause was the lychgate. Whenever the chance arose he would recheck its dimensions, its age (he even took a sample to date its wood) and, of course, every scrap of history he could glean online.

D I O'Connor's motive to find the truth was different. He remained haunted by the number of missing people he had been unable to track down.

However much he tried to think of an alternative, it was impossible to ignore that the last sightings of many had been in the vicinity of the lychgate. Despite his better judgement, he had spent hours watching that sinister portal at the dead of night. The only other person about at the same time had been a young man with a smartphone who always left as soon as he arrived.

The detective had also measured the lychgate, photographed it from every angle, and took soundings to see if there was a cavity beneath it. There was a space of sorts, but probably due to ancient footings rotting away.

D I O'Connor was preparing to slide into well deserved retirement with his much younger, attractive wife and join the bowls club, when he encountered that androgynous looking young man again, too busy tapping away at his smartphone as though just discovering a Pokémon point to notice him.

'Odd time to be raising electronic deities?' D I O'Connor observed non-judgementally. It was ten in the evening and a similar charge could have been made against him for loitering by the lychgate.

At first Dom was taken aback as though being caught out in some misdemeanour, then explained,

'This is a portal, you know.' He seemed to understand what he was talking about, though unsure whether he believed it.

'What? To the tunnels?'

'No idea, these readings say that there is some sort of different atmospheric "density" here.'

D I O'Connor was intrigued, but tried not to show it. 'Really?'

'Yeah. It's the last place some people were seen heading to before they disappeared, you know.'

D I O'Connor raised a non-committal eyebrow, so Dom went on, 'No trace of them at all. No bones, no clothes, no DNA.'

'What do you think happened to them?'

'Got to be a dimensional thing,' shrugged Dom. 'With quantum physics, anything is possible.'

'You think they're still alive?'

'Perhaps in some sort of limbo.'

The detective shuddered, though wasn't sure why.

He left the owner of the smartphone busily tapping away and returned home to the notes he had often studied about the disappearances.

Before he could start reading them he noticed the envelope on the mantelpiece addressed to him in his wife's hand. For a couple who had been married for over 25 years it was an unsettlingly formal way of making contact. He may have been a detective, well tuned to the behaviour of other people, but oblivious of what had been going on under his nose. There had never been any indication that Marion was having an affair. When the letter announced that she had run off with her much younger lover, it dropped like a bombshell.

The room spun as his world and all its sureties spiralled down into despair's whirlpool. The life he expected to end with a loving partner had been snatched away to diminish his very existence. All his hopes had been built around that marriage, even the decision not to allow children to intrude, only to have a few brief sentences declare that there was no such future.

As the detective toppled into an armchair, the notebooks containing details of the missing persons were swept onto the carpet.

Only then did he begin to understand.

All those disappeared people had faced similar traumas. There were many varying reasons, but without exception they had triggered the same soul destroying results.

D I O'Connor automatically pulled on his coat.

It was almost midnight when he reached the lychgate, the cemetery lamp silhouetting its pitched roof and ornate posts.

He stood gazing at it, not knowing why he was there, only that it was better than sitting at home waiting for the phone call that would never come.

Marion had gone for good. She had made that clear.

The feelings he could not express through years of self-control seemed to spill into the shadow of the lychgate and manifest themselves.

A tall shape formed in the arch and blocked out the cemetery light.

It might have been an angel - or demon - but had no wings, halo or fiery sword. It just hung there, a shimmering shadow, waiting for a response.

'Let me in...' the detective asked without realising he had spoken.

The spectre raised a phantom hand and beckoned him forward.

The lychgate became a portal of light.

D I O'Connor allowed it to envelope him.

When Dom returned the next day to confirm his findings, the readings had changed. The ones he had taken to be atmospheric pressure were now quite normal.

But there was something else.

Dom lowered his smartphone and stared at the shimmering air in the lychgate.

He could make out ghostly shapes, moving around and happily interacting in a strange, endless otherworld, but before he could remove his spectacles and wipe them, the mirage had gone.

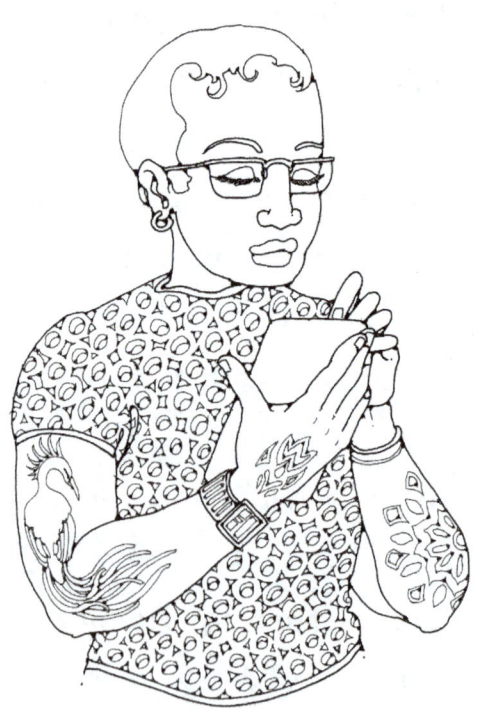

The Overgown

It was magic!

She opened her overgown to reveal a scene of forests and castles in the sky embroidered on its lining. It was an exquisite world filled with movement.

Then she quickly closed the overgown.

When it was opened again, the wonderful dimension had gone and was replaced with the island destinations Jim and Alice had flown to over the years.

How could this mystic in the sideshow of a rundown funfair know the places they had visited? Between them, this couple had generated more air miles and pollution than a head of state. And they had many more trips planned before their pension pots were eventually drained.

It was difficult to see what such a skilled illusionist was doing in these tawdry surroundings, and why was there no other audience in this small tent? Her performance was just for them. It was not only astonishing, but a little scary and Jim and Alice would have preferred some company.

The next time the illusionist opened her overgown some more countries they had visited were revealed, but not those places tourists snapped with their smartphones and posted on Facebook. Beyond those sites that attracted visitors were the slums, the scorched land of failed crops, and places where people lived on the brink of starvation.

Jim and Alice did not want to see any more, but another sweep of the overgown revealed burning forests which filled the tent with suffocating smoke.

Jim and Alice were not aware that the mysterious funfair was moving on. Roundabouts parents would not allow their children to ride, and a shooting gallery that had rifles with crooked sites no one would have dared pick up, were packed into their trailers before disappearing into the night.

The illusionist's tent folded itself like a huge piece of origami and flapped off into the moonlit sky.

Jim and Alice suddenly woke.

They were on a tropical island in a shack overlooking a turquoise sea.

Neither remembered booking a flight to this exotic location, and if they had they would have chosen a hotel.

The couple were so overwhelmed by the beauty of the place, they did not immediately notice that they were without luggage and dressed like the islanders further up the shore who were busily ferrying their worldly goods to higher ground.

Jim and Alice's shack was being lapped by the incoming tide. All they could think of was to save their passports. They should have been in their luggage...

Phantom Friend

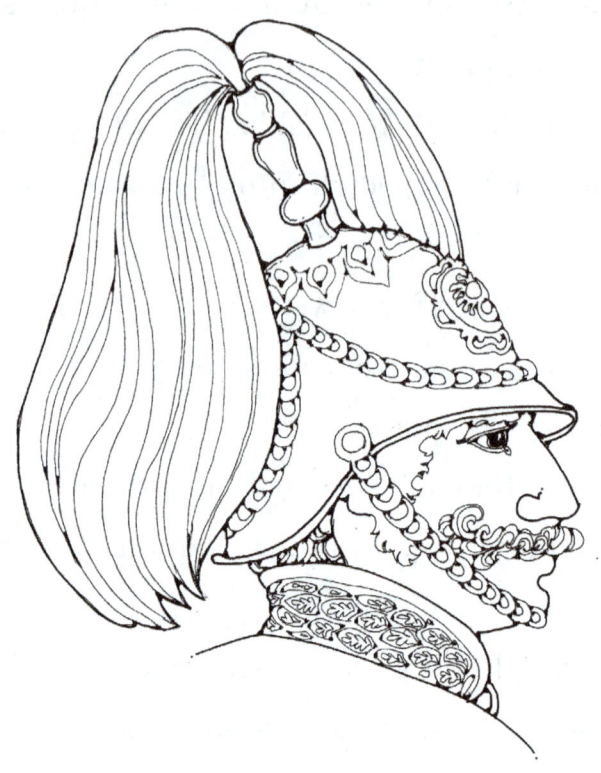

He had always been there, sitting beside Malcolm at the table and watching over his shoulder as his infant brain attempted multiplication.

The adults didn't mind back then: many children had invisible friends. But Malcolm was now 46, had three failed marriages, five children and one heart attack, probably brought on by his second divorce. Perhaps it was because of his phantom friend that he survived them all. Archie, invisible to everyone else, was his support and true soul mate.

No longer able to admit that he had a secret companion in the grown-up world, Malcolm became more and more dependent on the one friend he could talk to - though obviously not out loud. A dodgy heart was one thing, premature senility quite another.

There were moments of weakness when Malcolm wondered whether Archie should be confined to those other immature fantasies most young people dispense with at puberty. Giving him up, though, would have been worse than going without a cigarette. If it hadn't been for Archie he would still be smoking. When Malcolm needed him most, there he was, mirroring every thought like a doppelgänger, counselling and reassuring him.

This friend surely could not have been the creation of an infant's subconscious because, as Malcolm grew, so had Archie. Why hadn't his boyhood fantasy dreamt up someone more dashing, like a Victorian cavalry officer. (He had always been fascinated by them.) A perfect, bewhiskered gentleman, softly spoken with an archaic accent that could have only sprung from the pages of a Victorian edition of Punch, resplendent with plumed helmet and dangerously sharp sword.

But Archie was not the heroic type, very much like the person who had dreamt him up.

Malcolm sometimes wished, as he strolled with Penny, his Labrador, and in secret conversation with Archie that his phantom friend did wear a cavalry uniform and had a horse which he cared for like a high society wife. But Archie was far too open-minded to be that sort of Victorian, and his beliefs encompassed all religions with a degree of tolerance that made him and Malcolm such like minds. It was simply personal relationships he had problems with.

Then, one day, sitting on the fallen log that was his regular seat, Malcolm opened the treats he always gave his Labrador at that point.

But this time Archie reached out to take some.

Without thinking, Malcolm dropped some chocolate drops into his palm.

Archie offered them to Penny, who took him from his hand.

Malcolm suddenly realised what had happened.

The dog had no way of knowing Archie was only a phantom and chewed enthusiastically.

Malcolm nearly toppled from the log, but regained his balance in time. During a lifetime of being boon companions, it had never occurred to him to reach out and touch Archie. Malcolm's subconscious knew that he really wasn't there, so why would he?

He slowly extended his hand and laid it on the soft fabric of Archie's shirt. It felt like silk.

Malcolm must have been having a stroke. But Penny was unlikely to be sharing the same hallucination.

Archie remained unfazed at the empathic bond engulfing them.

'Just who are you?' murmured Malcolm.

'My name is really Alex, but I much prefer Archie.'

Why, after all these years, had Archie waited to reveal his true nature?

'There is a letter waiting for you. It will explain,' Archie said.

How could anyone else know about the secret companion Malcolm had never mentioned to another living soul?

But they did.

Aunt Veronica, older sister of Malcolm's long dead mother, had at last gone back to the great maker she so fervently believed in as a devout Christian. She was determined that some truths should never remain buried, and had decided that her nephew had the right to know what had been kept from him since birth.

He apparently had an identical twin who only survived long enough to be christened.

His name was Alex.

As Malcolm read her letter, he became aware that his lifelong companion was no longer there. Like Eve's apple, knowledge had robbed him of the innocence that kept Archie alive.

Silver, Silver Everywhere

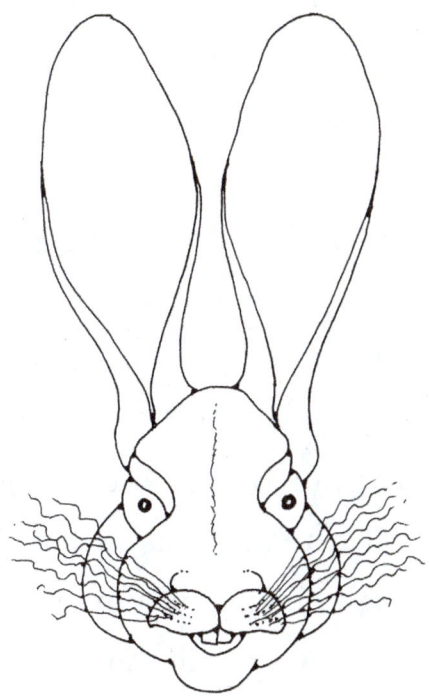

It shimmered, flowed and described glittering scrolls in the crisp air; a quicksilver blanket covering everything. Then, just as rapidly as it had appeared, it was gone.

Perhaps this was one optical illusion too far.

Being a genius, Sangeeta didn't think that she had overreached herself, though perhaps limits would need to be put on her research. In the wrong hands it could start a war.

The multiple 3-D projectors were powered down and the local wildlife poked apprehensive noses, paws and beaks from burrows and nests. Being chromed without warning was enough to unnerve the toughest carnivore.

Immersing the immediate region in reflective hues had not been Sangeeta's primary intention. The research was into how to extend the growing season by illuminating crops at night using powerful, low-power projectors. But then she found out too late that the metallic side effect had attracted the military funding that was now backing the project. Being able to turn cardboard missiles and their launchers into gleaming metal long enough for enemy satellites to be fooled could buy valuable time from their point of view. Growing anything eco-friendly didn't enter into it. The sooner that Sangeeta's project became viable enough to find different backers the better. No one in her team wanted the invention to become a weapon of war.

But it was too late - the government took over her department and compelled everyone to sign the Official Secrets Act.

Granville refused and started to upload the sorry saga onto the Internet. Before he could add any more, he and his blog disappeared - to where, no one knew.

After a nerve-racking pause, Sangeeta was given instructions to simulate multiple plywood tanks, missiles and other weaponry across the world into metal. Why, she had no idea. No war or invasion was imminent as far as anyone knew. Perhaps Granville did, but chose not to endanger anyone else by telling them. There had been rumours on the World Wide Web that aliens were trying to make contact, and it would have made some sort of sense from the military's point of view if the planet could show that they were battle ready.

Sangeeta doubted that aliens with the technology to travel the galaxy would have been fooled for one moment by her invention. But, not having Granville's determination to stand up to the authorities, her team set to work.

Shortly into the frenetic project, Granville turned up without warning. All those who had known him sensed that there was something wrong in the considered way he spoke instead of the words tumbling out as they usually did. Yes, the authorities had assured him, an alien spaceship was trying to make contact and they needed to be prepared.

Until then, because she didn't believe it, Sangeeta had been persuaded to follow the plan.

Now, everything had changed. Surely if an alien wanted to invade they would have done so immediately and not waited weeks for these puny primates to get used to the idea that they were not alone in the Universe.

After researching as much as she could using the computer of a friend able to bypass the regional servers being blocked, Granville's revelation was confirmed. Sangeeta was convinced that if there was an alien out there, its mission involved nothing more threatening than curiosity. But all the asteroid tracking stations, ground telescopes and satellites were now only accessible to the planet wide authorities preparing for invasion.

With everyone who might have been willing to make friendly contact locked out, Sangeeta could see a terrifying scenario loom. What if her invention created the illusion that the planet was hostile? Surely, however benign the alien's intentions, the show of battle readiness could provoke an understandable reaction. If there was a network of friendly civilisations out there, the last thing they would tolerate was an evolving species prepared to do battle before anyone had the chance to say 'hello'.

At the dead of night, Sangeeta used her security pass to unobtrusively slip into the project's control room. It was from there all the installations across the planet were primed to be activated as soon as the authorities responded to the alien's repeated attempts at first contact.

The reprogramming took hours. The most difficult thing was slipping out without anyone suspecting a few crucial elements had been changed.

When the acknowledgment to the alien's many greetings was at last sent a huge spacecraft slipped from the dimension concealing it and filled the sky.

Sangeeta's team were ordered to set in motion the battle ready illusion.

It took longer than anticipated and the planet held its breath, half expecting a bolt from the sky to eliminate all life forms on the planet.

At last the military hardware was illuminated so brightly it lit up the world.

But it was not with a metallic, menacing gleam.

Paisley patterns of every hue swirled across the war machinery and cardboard troops. The pinks, yellows, blues, greens and gold were reflected onto the clouds and filled large stretches of the blue Earth with welcoming, rotating hues of every colour.

Not even an alien could have mistaken that for a hostile act.